OLIVIA™
Wishes on a Star

adapted by Tina Gallo
based on the screenplay "Meteor Mania" written by Scott Gray
illustrated by Jared Osterhold

Simon Spotlight
New York   London   Toronto   Sydney   New Delhi

Based on the TV series OLIVIA™ as seen on Nickelodeon™

SIMON SPOTLIGHT
An imprint of Simon & Schuster Children's Publishing Division
1230 Avenue of the Americas, New York, New York 10020
First Simon Spotlight paperback edition November 2014
OLIVIA™ Ian Falconer Ink Unlimited, Inc. and © 2014 Ian Falconer and Classic Media, LLC.
For information about special discounts for bulk purchases, please contact
Simon & Schuster Special Sales at 1-866-506-1949 or business@simonandschuster.com.
Manufactured in the United States of America 1014 LAK
1 2 3 4 5 6 7 8 9 10
ISBN 978-1-4814-1769-3
ISBN 978-1-4814-1770-9 (eBook)

Olivia was sitting quietly in her classroom when Mrs. Hogenmuller said she had an exciting announcement.

"Something very special is happening tonight, class!" she said. "Do you know what that is?"

"Yes! It's spaghetti night at my house!" Olivia cheered.

"Mmm, that is special, Olivia, but that's not what I meant," Mrs. Hogenmuller said with a smile. "There's a meteor shower tonight!"

Harold made a face. "I don't like showers," he said. "I like baths."

"A meteor shower isn't a real shower, Harold," Mrs. Hogenmuller explained. "It's rocks and dust in outer space burning across the sky like fireworks! Some folks call this dazzling display 'falling stars.'" She held up a laptop so the class could see a video of falling stars.

"Wow!" Olivia said. "That's so cool!"

Mrs. Hogenmuller continued. "What's more, if you see a falling star and make a wish, some say it might come true! So I hope all your parents will let you stay up late to watch it."

Olivia whispered to Julian. "No problem. My parents will let me stay up. I'll just use my 'cute face!'" Olivia tilted her head and smiled at Julian. She made a very cute face at him.

That night while everyone was enjoying their spaghetti dinner, Olivia told her family about the meteor shower.

"So can I stay up? Please?" Olivia tilted her head and made the same cute face she had made at Julian.

Olivia's dad thought for a moment and then turned to her mom. "A meteor shower really is an amazing thing to see. . . ."

Olivia made her cutest face ever! "We can all make wishes!" she begged.
"Pleeeease?"

"Pleeease?" Dad repeated.

Even Ian stopped eating spaghetti long enough to join in. "Pleeease?" Ian asked.

Mom laughed. "Well, how can I resist those faces? Okay, the whole family will stay up and watch the meteor shower together. It will be fun!"

"Yay!" Olivia cheered.

Olivia jumped up from her chair. "Come on, Ian. We've got decorating to do!"
Mom and Dad stared at Olivia, confused.

"Decorating for what?" Mom asked.

"For our big falling star party, what else?" Olivia said. "Let's go!"

Olivia and Ian looked through Olivia's trunk to see what they could use. Olivia held up each item and then tossed it aside if it wasn't good for the theme of the party. "A puppet? No. A jester hat? No." Olivia tossed them aside. Then she pulled out a glow-in-the-dark planet mobile and a sheriff's badge.

"Planets, stars . . . perfect!" she said.

Ian blew loudly on a bagpipe. Olivia jumped.

"Aaah! No bagpipes, Ian!" she said.

A little while later, Olivia was in the kitchen, searching through all the cabinets.
"Olivia, please explain," Mom said.
"Chef Olivia is looking for the perfect snack for Falling Star Night," Olivia said
"I have just the thing," Mom told Olivia.

Mom opened the refrigerator and took out some fruit. She showed it to Olivia.
"It's called star fruit," Mom explained. "It's delicious, and when you cut it . . ."
Mom cut the fruit in half and held it up for Olivia to see.
"It looks exactly like a star!" Olivia exclaimed. "It's perfect. And I know how to
make it even perfect-er!" She grabbed a sack of powdered sugar and sprinkled it
all over the star fruit.
"Powdered sugar?" Mom asked.
"Stardust!" Olivia said proudly.

While they were waiting to see the falling stars, the whole family had fun at Olivia's falling star party. Olivia taped a drawing of a falling star to the wall. She blindfolded Dad and gave him a paper comet tail with a piece of sticky tape on the end of it. Olivia spun Dad around.

"Whoaa!" said Dad. He was dizzy!

"Okay, now, pin the tail on the falling star," Olivia instructed.

"No problem," Dad said.

But Dad stumbled into the wall, reached out, and taped the tail on Edwin!

"Got it!" Dad said.

Dad took off his blindfold. Edwin yowled.

"Edwin! You've grown two tails!" Dad said.

"Okay, Ian, it's your turn," Olivia said. But when she turned around to blindfold Ian, he was asleep on the couch!

"Ian's asleep!" Olivia cried.

"He's tired. I am, too," Mom said. "Maybe we should all go to sleep and watch the meteor shower on the news tomorrow."

"Don't worry. I'll wake Ian up," Olivia said. "With a little help from . . .
the Tickle Monster!"

Olivia moved next to Ian and started tickling him.

"Kitchy kitchy koo!" Olivia sang out as she tickled Ian.

"Stop it!" Ian cried. He was still half asleep. Then as he opened his eyes and
stared at Olivia, he realized what had happened. "Ooh, thanks, Olivia," he
said.

"Thank you for waking up!" Olivia said. She turned to say something to Mom
and Dad when she noticed Dad had his eyes closed. He was snoring!

"Oh no, now Dad's asleep!" Olivia gasped. She rushed to his side and started tickling him, the same way she tickled Ian.

"Kitchy kitchy koo!" Olivia said as she tickled Dad. But Dad didn't wake up.

"When he's this tired," Mom told Olivia, "the only thing that wakes him is the light from the morning sun."

"Well, if light wakes Dad up," Olivia proclaimed with a smile, "let there be light!"

Olivia ran and got flashlights for herself, Ian, and Mom.

"Three, two, one—lights!" Olivia shouted.

They all clicked their flashlights on at the same time, right at Dad. He jumped up right away.

"I'm late for work!" Dad shouted. "Oops. Guess I fell asleep."

"That's okay, Dad," Olivia said. "Now I know how to keep you awake. Thanks, Mom."

A few minutes later Mom snored. And then Dad snored too!
Now everyone was asleep! Mom, Dad, Ian—even Perry and Edwin were asleep!
"I wish there was a way to keep everyone awake, all at once," Olivia said to Baby
William. "Wait a minute . . . there is! But it's going to take a whole lot of tape."

Olivia left for a moment and returned in a "wake up" costume! She had a flashlight on her hat and horns on her feet. She had a wooden spoon in one hand and a long feather in the other. She had a pot tied to her waist to bang with the spoon. And finally, she had the bagpipes tucked under her arm. "It's showtime," Olivia said.

Olivia hopped up and down while she banged her spoon, aimed her headlight at Dad, and tickled Ian with the feather. Then she blew the bagpipes. Everyone woke up with a start. "How can such a little girl make such a big noise?" Mom said.

"Easy!" Olivia told her. "With a wake-up dance!"

"I like it," Dad said. "It's catchy."

Then everyone danced!

Suddenly Dad looked at his watch. "The meteor shower is starting," he said. "Time to go outside!"

Everyone rushed to the backyard to watch falling stars.

"There goes one!" shouted Mom, pointing.

Olivia and Ian gasped.

Just at that moment, an entire field of falling stars lit up the sky!

Everyone cheered!

Later on, Mom tucked Olivia into bed.

"The falling stars were beautiful," Olivia said. "It was the perfect night."

"What did you wish for?" Mom asked.

Olivia gasped. "Oh no! I was so excited I forgot to make a wish. But it's okay.
I'm just happy everyone got to see the meteor shower."

Mom smiled. "Good night, Olivia."

Olivia was just about to fall asleep when something caught her eye. A single falling star soared by her window.

Olivia smiled to herself.

"I wish everyone in my family will get what they wished for tonight," she whispered softly.

Soon she was asleep, watching falling stars in her dreams.